OUT OF THIS WORLD

Out of This World is published by Stone Arch Books,
A Capstone Imprint
1710 Roe Crest Drive
North Mankato, Minnesota 56003
www.mycapstone.com

Library of Congress Cataloging-in-Publication Data
Names: Bean, Raymond, author.
Title: First family in space / by Raymond Bean.
Description: North Mankato, Minnesota : Stone Arch Books, an imprint of
Capstone Press, [2016] | Series: Out of this world, out of this world | Summary:
Ten-year-old Starr, the middle child in her family, is not thrilled to learn that they
are all moving again: she is sick of changing schools, and leaving friends behind--but
this time the move is to a space station in orbit around the Earth.
Identifiers: LCCN 2016013786| ISBN 9781496536174 (library binding) | ISBN
9781496536211 (pbk.) | ISBN 9781496536297 (ebook (pdf))
Subjects: LCSH: Space stations--Juvenile fiction. | Moving, Household--Juvenile
fiction. | Middle-born children--Juvenile fiction. | Brothers and sisters--Juvenile
fiction. | Families--Juvenile fiction. | Outer space--Juvenile fiction. | CYAC: Space
stations--Fiction. | Moving, Household--Fiction. | Brothers and sisters--Fiction. |
Family life--Fiction. | Outer space--Fiction.
Classification: LCC PZ7.B3667 Fi 2016 | DDC 813.6 [Fic] --dc23
LC record available at https://lccn.loc.gov/2016013786

Illustrated by: Matthew Vimislik
Designer: Veronica Scott

OUT OF THIS WORLD

FiRST FAMiLY iN SPACE

by Raymond Bean

STONE ARCH BOOKS
a capstone imprint

TABLE OF CONTENTS

Chapter 1

GOOD MORNING?

I'd been looking forward to my best friend Allison's eleventh birthday party for months. She and I had some awesome plans. Her mom let us order a big bunch of balloons. We even handwrote all the invitations together on fancy paper. It was supposed to be the best party ever.

So when my parents walked into my bedroom one morning and told me my family was moving, I was devastated.

"We can't move!" I insisted. "Allison's party is in three weeks!"

"Starr, I've been offered a job that's too good to pass up," Mom said.

"It's going to be an amazing new adventure for all of us," my dad added, trying to convince me.

I could tell that their minds were already made up. They weren't asking me; they were telling me. It had happened before. I knew the drill.

My mom is a super-successful scientist/astronaut/pilot/genius, and she's pretty much awesome at everything. She has more trophies and awards than my two brothers and I have put together.

She's so into space that my brothers and I have space-related names. Apollo is thirteen and thinks he's the coolest thing since ice cubes. Cosmo just turned five. If you ask me, he *is* the coolest thing since ice cubes. Most people call him Cos for short, but I usually call him Cozzie because it's cute.

My mom is *always* getting new job offers. When she takes a new job, we end up having to change schools and make new friends. So far we've lived in Australia, Japan, England, and the United States, and I'm only ten! I figure that if we keep moving at this rate, I'll probably live in every country on Earth at least once.

Dad's a documentary filmmaker. We had to move once for his job a long time ago, but it's Mom's jobs that keep us moving the most.

"Where are we going this time?" I asked, feeling defeated. Anywhere else would be bad, but I hoped it would at least be close enough to still see Allison. I've had to leave friends before, but she's by far the best friend I've ever had.

"You couldn't guess if I gave you a million tries," Mom said, snuggling up next to me.

"Will I have to change schools?" I knew the answer, but I asked anyway. There was always a new school.

"You'll have to change more than your school, honey,"

Dad said, sitting on the edge of my bed. He gently placed his hand on my knee.

Oh boy, I thought, *this is going to be a doozy.*

Mom smiled cautiously as she said, "Starr, we're moving to space!"

I stared at them blankly and said, "I've never heard of a city called Space."

"We're not moving to a *city* called Space!" Dad exclaimed, as if he were trying to sell me something. "We're moving *to* SPACE! As in outer space: the final frontier, the great beyond! I'll film our whole adventure. The first family in space! It'll be my best film yet!"

I sat up. "Are you guys kidding?"

"No, Starr, this isn't a joke," Mom said softly. "It's always been my dream to live in space."

"But what if it's not *my* dream?" I asked.

"Well, sometimes you have to make changes in your life to support the ones you love," Dad said. "It's called making a sacrifice."

"I don't know if I'd think of it as a sacrifice," Mom added, glancing at Dad. "Think of it as more of an opportunity. Many people have been to space, but we'll be the first *family* to ever go to space. It's the chance of a lifetime!"

"When do we leave?" I asked awkwardly. Tears welled up in my eyes. One rolled down my cheek and landed on the bedsheet, making a circle that reminded me of Earth. I already felt a million miles away. "Can I still go to Allison's party?" I asked.

They glanced at each other again, and I knew the answer.

"Oh, Starr, I'm so sorry," Mom said. "We're leaving before her party."

"Missing the party, moving again, and leaving my best friend? That's some sacrifice."

Chapter 2

MOVING DAY

About a week later, a huge truck backed down our driveway early in the morning. Movers packed and loaded everything we owned. Allison had come over to spend some time with me while the movers worked and Mom and Dad scurried around taking care of last-minute things. Apollo and Cozzie built a fort on the front lawn out of extra cardboard moving boxes, but Allison and I didn't feel like playing with them. We drew on the sidewalk with chalk instead.

"I don't want you to leave," Allison said.

"That makes two of us," I added.

"I still don't understand how you can be moving to space? Is that even possible?"

"For my mom, anything is possible," I said.

"Are you going in a rocket ship or something?"

"We're going to live at a training place in the desert first. After training, yeah, we'll blast off in some kind of spaceship. I'm pretty scared about it," I shared.

"My mom says you'll be the first girl ever in space."

"There have been plenty of girls in space — Valentina Tereshkova, Sally Ride, Sunita Williams . . .," I said.

"They were women. You'll be the first *girl*. You'll probably become famous and forget all about me."

"You're my best friend," I said. "I'll never forget you."

"So, when was the last time you talked with any of the kids from your last school?" she asked.

I thought about it and couldn't remember. "It's been a long time," I admitted.

"Exactly! You're going to move, have this amazing

new life, and forget all about me."

"That's not true. You know," I said, trying to change the subject, "we'll be in space on your birthday, in two weeks. Maybe we can set up a video call, and I can sing 'Happy Birthday' to you from space! Mom and Dad gave me my own phone so I can keep in touch. Mom said there will be special new technology, so we'll be able to make calls and text just like we do on Earth."

"We'll see," she answered, looking sad. "I'm going to be really busy with my party and everything."

We didn't talk much after that. I felt like crying, and I'm pretty sure she did too. Allison even called her mom to pick her up early.

"Is everything okay?" Mom asked as Allison's mom drove away from our house.

"No," I answered. "I don't think she wants to be friends with someone who lives in space."

Mom didn't say anything. She just gave me a hug.

That afternoon, when the moving truck pulled away,

I couldn't help but think that I'd trade everything in that truck if it meant I could stay.

We went back in our house one last time. Dad marked our height and the date on the wooden molding inside the kitchen pantry. He'd done it in every house we lived in, which was pretty silly because every time we moved he had to start the measurements all over again. He said to smile and took a picture of me in front of the chart. I forced the best smile I could manage, but it wasn't easy.

Chapter 3

ARE WE ON MARS?

We loaded into the car for the long drive to the desert. Since my parents had sold Mom's minivan, my brothers and I crammed into the backseat of Dad's little four-door. My brothers didn't seem as upset about the move as I did.

I texted Allison as we pulled out of the driveway: *Leaving now. Talk soon.*

I checked every few seconds to see if she'd texted me. I was so distracted I forgot to look back at the house one last time. A few long minutes went by before she finally texted: *Good luck.*

I couldn't believe that was it. I thought we were best friends. *Good luck? That's all she has to say?* I thought.

A few hours into our drive, Cozzie turned to me and asked, "Will there be aliens in space?"

"No, I don't think there are aliens in space, Cozzie."

"Have you ever been there?" he asked.

"No."

"Then how do you know? There could be billions and zillions of them up there and you wouldn't even know it."

"He has a point," Apollo said, smirking. Apollo liked to give Cozzie and me a hard time every chance he got. I always felt like he was making fun of us, but sometimes it was hard to tell.

"Don't listen to him," I said to Cozzie.

"I think there are aliens," Apollo added. "I just hope they don't want to eat my brain."

"Why would they want to eat *your* brain?" I asked.

"I don't want aliens to eat *my* brains," Cozzie whimpered.

Mom glanced into the rearview mirror, glaring at

Apollo. "Why would you tell your little brother there are brain-eating aliens?"

"I saw it in a movie once."

"No one is going to eat your brain," Dad reassured Cozzie.

I texted Allison while they bickered: *Cozzie's worried that aliens are going to eat his brain. Do you believe in aliens?*

No reply. I must have checked a thousand times before falling asleep.

We drove all night, and at sunrise, Dad and I were the only ones awake. I felt like I'd been asleep forever. We were deep in the desert. Cactuses and sand dunes stretched out as far as I could see. The sand looked reddish-orange in the early morning sunlight.

I checked to see if Allison had gotten back to me. She had. It read: *Okay.*

Okay? I thought. *Okay! What is "Okay" supposed to mean?* She hadn't even answered my question.

I looked out the window and in the distance spotted a few buildings. They were solid white and seemed to glow in the sunlight. As we got closer, I could see a thin dirt road leading toward the buildings.

Dad turned, sending dust clouds up behind the car as it crunched and bumped along. I was surprised that no one woke up.

"Dad, do you think it's fair that Allison is mad at me for moving?" I asked.

"What makes you think she's mad at you?" he asked.

"I can just tell."

"She's probably just sad and having a hard time dealing with it."

I was quiet for a while. Dad was probably right, but it didn't make it any easier.

As we got closer to the buildings, I could make out what looked like large airplanes. They were like giant birds resting in a nest. Dad and I made eye contact in the rearview mirror.

"Spaceships," he whispered.

I could see what looked like runways stretching off into the distance. They were dark black and as wide as a highway.

"Is it an airport?" I asked.

"A space port," Dad said, and for the first time, it all felt very real. We were actually moving to space.

The car came to a stop and Cozzie woke. "Are we on Mars?" he asked, rubbing his eyes.

I smiled for the first time in a while. "No, Cozzie. We're in the desert."

"Have you seen any aliens yet?" he asked.

"We're still on Earth," Apollo said, stretching. "The aliens are up there," he said, pointing to the sky.

"There are no aliens," Mom said, now awake too and sounding annoyed.

I opened my window, and the desert heat poured in like invisible lava. A woman appeared in the window and startled Cozzie and me. Large, round glasses covered half of her face. Snow white hair curled and twisted to her waist. She was old, but a young-looking sort of old. "I'm sorry. Did I surprise you?" she asked.

"I thought you were an alien," Cozzie said.

"Do I look like an alien?" she asked.

Mom got out of the car and hugged the woman. "No, not at all."

Apollo shrugged, as if to say that she did look like an alien, and I gave him a nudge.

I got out of the car.

"Starr, this is Mrs. Sosa," Mom said. "She owns the space program."

"Hi, Mrs. Sosa. I don't think you look like an alien," I said, giving her the most adorable smile I could manage.

"Well, thanks," she replied with a smile of her own. "You must be Starr."

"Mrs. Sosa, it's fantastic to see you again," said Dad, as he climbed out of the car. "Would you please point me in the direction of the nearest bathroom?"

Cozzie stepped from the car and started squirming like a worm. "I've got to go!" he announced.

Mrs. Sosa chuckled and pointed to the nearest building. Dad picked him up and raced toward it. Apollo followed close behind. He looked a little squirmy too.

"Looks like you made it just in time," Mrs. Sosa said, giving me a wink. "Starr, I'm absolutely thrilled to finally meet you. Your mother has told me so much about you."

Did she tell you that I didn't want to move? I thought. I bit my lip because I didn't want to be rude.

"Moving is hard. How are you holding up?"

"I don't know," I said. "I think I'm going to really miss home."

"Of course you will, but I think you'll learn to love this new adventure. The work we're doing here is historic. Our goal is to create a vacation experience in space. Space travelers will train here much like your family is going to do. Then, when they're ready, they'll travel to the space station and stay with your family and a small crew. When your brothers return from their little potty break, how about I show you all around a bit?"

I smiled. "That sounds fun."

Chapter 4

ZERO GRAVITY

Dad and the boys returned from the bathroom, and Mrs. Sosa led us into another building. I texted Allison back as I walked: *We're in the desert. I wish you could see it.*

"Starr, please stop playing with your phone," Mom requested. "It's a little rude."

"I was just texting Allison," I replied.

We followed Mrs. Sosa into a strange room. Blinking and bleeping computers filled one side. A few people worked at the computers. The other side looked like the inside of a regular house. I could see a kitchen and a living room. A high glass wall separated the two sides. Huge metal doors stood at the center of the glass. Mrs. Sosa stopped in front of the doors.

I noticed a zero on one door and a letter "G" on the other. "Behind these doors," she said excitedly, "is one of the coolest rooms in the world." Her dark eyes widened even more. "Would you like to go inside?"

"YES!" Cozzie shouted. If he were a puppy, his tail would have been wagging.

"Me too!" said Mrs. Sosa. "But, first, I have a question. Do you know what gravity is?"

"It's the sauce you put on meat," Cozzie answered.

Apollo laughed, and I could tell Cozzie didn't know if he was laughing at him.

"I think it was a fine guess," Mrs. Sosa said, standing up for Cozzie. I could tell Mrs. Sosa thought Cozzie was adorable, which made me instantly like her.

Unfortunately, this show of kindness also reminded me of Allison. I checked again to see if she had replied.

Mrs. Sosa must have noticed I was distracted because she asked, "Starr, do you know what gravity is?"

Cozzie said, "Starr knows everything."

Mom gently slipped the phone from my hand.

"I don't know everything, but I do know that 'gravy' and 'gravity' sound a lot alike," I said. "Even though they sound similar, they have different meanings. *Gravy* is delicious, and *gravity* is what pulls us to Earth. Without it, we'd float away."

"Correct," Mrs. Sosa said. "In space, objects pull on each other. Larger objects pull with more force than smaller objects. When we leave Earth and go to space, the force of gravity changes. This room may look like an ordinary kitchen and living room, but it's actually the only simulator in the world that can create Zero-G."

"I know what that is!" Apollo said. "It's like when astronauts float around in space."

"Like bubbles?" Cozzie asked.

"Yes, kind of like bubbles," Mrs. Sosa said. "Apollo,

you're exactly right. Zero-G is what astronauts experience when they go to space. Would you kids like to give it a try?"

We all nodded excitedly.

After Apollo, Cozzie, and I put on special space suits, we were ready to try. I was surprised that my suit was purple. The rest were all blue. I knew Mom had probably ordered it specially for me.

"Purple is my favorite color," I told Mrs. Sosa.

"I know," she said.

Mom winked at me and smiled.

"Did Allison text back?" I asked her. Mom was still keeping my phone safe.

"Be present, Starr," Mom reminded me. She was right. I was letting my worries about Allison distract me from what I was about to do.

"Can I go first?" I asked.

"Of course you can," Mrs. Sosa said.

"Why do you get to go first?" Apollo asked bluntly.

"Ladies first," Cozzie said, bowing.

Apollo made a stink face.

"Ladies first, it is," Mrs. Sosa said. She continued, "Zero-G is a little strange to get used to, but you'll get the hang of it. We won't keep you in there too long. You've had a long trip and you guys need some rest."

"You don't have to do this if you're too tired," Mom said.

"I'm okay. I want to do it," I replied.

Mrs. Sosa opened the door and I walked inside. She handed me a helmet that looked a lot like a bike helmet, helped me strap it on, and then closed the door. "We'll turn on the simulator. I'd like you to try to make your way from one side of the kitchen to the other and then back again."

"No problem." *This is going to be a piece of cake,* I thought.

"The glass is too thick for you to hear us, but we'll be able to communicate through this microphone," she said.

"You should feel it start any second. Wait for it."

My phone blinked in Mom's hand. I knew it was Allison. *Be present,* I thought.

I waited for something to happen, trying not to wonder what Allison wrote. Cozzie waved to me from the other side of the glass. I raised my hand to wave back, and that's when it happened.

One second I stood on solid ground just like I had every other day of my life, and the next my feet simply rose off the floor. It was kind of like I was falling. My stomach felt like it did the time I rode the Scream Train roller coaster at Adventure Blast. The coaster takes you way up high in the air, where you can see out over the entire park, and then rolls you over the other side headed straight down. I remember lifting right off my seat, and the only thing holding me in was my harness. I also remember feeling like my stomach fell right out of my body and not being able to breathe. This was a lot like that.

I moved my arms as if I were swimming. My heart thumped in my chest with excitement and fear.

"Try holding onto something for a moment until you get used to it," Mrs. Sosa said.

I held onto a metal bar bolted to the wall. On the Scream Train, the feeling of falling went away after a few seconds. This was different. The feeling didn't go away. I was confused because my body felt one thing — I was falling; but my eyes saw something else — I was floating. I'd never experienced anything like it. I slowly got used to it and could appreciate that I was no longer standing on the ground. I floated like an astronaut in space!

I could see Cozzie hopping up and down.

"When you think you're ready, give a push off," Mrs. Sosa encouraged.

I gripped the bar tightly. My feet continued to move up toward the ceiling. With a soft push, I floated slowly across the room. More metal bars that reminded me of monkey bars lined the ceiling. I grabbed hold of one to stop from hitting the wall and realized it was lined with soft foam.

"Great job!" Mrs. Sosa said. "Those are stabilizer bars. They're attached to the walls, floor, and ceiling to give you something to hold onto. You're doing great. Now try a somersault. Nothing crazy, simply start to roll and then let yourself go. If you need to stop, just grab a bar."

Mrs. Sosa seemed like she was having as much fun as I was. I pushed off the bar and grabbed my knees like I would when flipping off a diving board. My body slowly spun in two full circles. It was like a dream.

"Straighten out," Mrs. Sosa instructed.

I let go of my knees and pushed my legs out straight. I floated toward the door. "Grab hold of the bar on the wall," she told me. "We're going to shut it off. Get ready."

I did as she said and, just like that, Earth pulled me back to where I belonged. My knees trembled from the excitement.

She opened the door. "Well?"

"That was the best thing ever!" I exclaimed.

It was so fun that if I live to be one hundred years old, I bet I'll remember it.

Chapter 5

WATER BALLS

Mom handed me my phone while Apollo had his turn.
Allison's text said: *I'm kind of busy planning my party. I
can't keep texting you back.*

"She's mad at me alright," I told Dad, showing him the
text.

"Give her some time," he said. "Try to enjoy where we
are right now. Allison will come around."

Over the next few days, we trained pretty much all
the time. I tried as hard as I could not to think about
Allison. I wanted to call her and text her, but I didn't.

We spent as much time in Zero-G as we were allowed. Apollo and I even made up a game called Cozzie Ball. It was like a combination of basketball and soccer, with Cozzie as the ball. He'd pull his knees in toward his chest like he was doing a cannonball dive into a pool. We'd take turns passing him to each other. He floated in the air, spinning like a space rock. In full gravity, I could hardly lift him off the ground, but in Zero-G, I could spin him on one finger.

We were in the middle of a close game when I noticed Mrs. Sosa outside the simulator. I was surprised to see that she had a girl with her. She looked about my age.

The engineer shut down the simulator for a moment. Mrs. Sosa and the girl came in after we had floated down.

"Starr, this is my granddaughter, Tia," she said.

Tia had long, black hair and glasses that covered most of her face. She looked a lot like a young Mrs. Sosa. I could tell they were related.

Before I could say anything, Tia put on her helmet and asked the engineer to shut the door and turn the Zero-G back on. Once we were floating, she pulled a few bottles of water from a compartment next to her and handed one to each of us. "Have a drink," she instructed.

I thought this was weird, but I *was* kind of thirsty. When I twisted the cap, the water floated out of the bottle, forming floating water balls! Tia poked one with her finger and it split into two smaller balls. They wiggled in front of me like floating Jell-O. Tia had clearly done this before.

"Quick, eat them!" she said. She gulped one up.

I opened my mouth, and Apollo floated past, stealing it away. Annoyed, I twisted the cap off my bottle again, allowing some more of the water to float out. The water floated in the air like soap bubbles. This time, I didn't waste a second and I sucked one into my mouth. I had never experienced anything like it.

After finishing all the water, Apollo and Cozzie played

in the living room, but I stayed in the kitchen with Tia and Mrs. Sosa.

"Wasn't that amazing?" Tia asked, floating upside down in front of me.

"It was!" I said, pushing gently off a stabilizer bar so that I was upside down too.

"Are you and Tia coming up to space with us?" I asked Mrs. Sosa.

"Tia and her parents live with me here at my space port. The plan is for you and Tia to become partners. Over the next few months, you'll work together to help other kids transition from Earth to space. She'll train the kids here on Earth and prepare them for life on the space station, and you'll work with them once they're on board."

"You're the lucky one," Tia said, staring at me. "I'll be stuck down here on boring Earth while you're up in the space station having all the fun."

"Tia, we've talked about this," Mrs. Sosa said in a warning tone. Tia frowned.

Great, I thought, *another person to be mad at me.*

"Have you been to space already?" I asked.

"No. I know everything there is to know about space, but Grandma won't let *me* go."

"I believe it's important that the first kids who travel to space go with their family," Mrs. Sosa said. "You'll have a chance soon enough. Since Starr's mom is the astronaut, she and her family will be the first ones."

Tia frowned.

"How long will people stay up in space?" I asked.

"At first, only a few days. But, as we learn more, we'll be able to take space travelers on longer and longer journeys."

"So it's like a vacation in space?" I asked.

"A space-cation," Tia said, and I giggled. She tried to hide it, but she soon giggled too. However, I couldn't tell if Tia liked me or not. She seemed nice, but she also seemed full of jealousy.

I hadn't thought about Allison much that afternoon. It was only after dinner that I started to feel sad again.

So that night I called Allison and was surprised that she answered. I told her about all the cool things we were doing. But she didn't sound that interested.

"There's even another girl here. Her name is Tia."

"Is she your new best friend?" Allison asked.

"Of course not, you'll always be my best friend."

"If you were my best friend, you never would have moved away."

I couldn't think of anything to say, but that night in bed I kept thinking about what she'd said. I didn't realize that best friends had to live next to each other in order to *stay* best friends. If that were the case, who would be my best friend in space?

Chapter 6

NO ALIENS . . . YET, BUT I'M LOOKING

One week had passed, and it was the day we were scheduled to blast off. We woke up so early it was still dark out. Mrs. Sosa and Tia came to see us before we left.

"Keep me updated," Tia said. "I want to know everything! And since I can't go . . ."

Mrs. Sosa looked annoyed and said, "Be patient and you'll have your chance too. Let's be happy for Starr."

"Have an amazing flight," Tia said to me, still eyeing Mrs. Sosa. "Let me know if you need anything."

"Will do," I said uncomfortably.

Before I knew it, we were in our space suits, loaded on the ship and prepared for liftoff. Apollo and I buckled into our seats, and Mom and Dad made sure Cozzie was strapped in safely between us. I reached over and held his hand. Mom and Dad sat in the front and the kids were in the back. Mom was in the captain's seat.

The top of the ship was clear glass. I could see the blue sky above and the start of the sunrise filling the sky with light.

The spaceship rolled down the runway just like an airplane. We picked up speed for a few seconds, and then we were off the ground and flying.

The ship immediately started climbing higher and higher. I kept my eyes looking down at the desert below. I could make out the roads. They were like veins running along the desert surface. Soon the roads blended with

the sand and it was only desert. I trembled a little with excitement, or maybe fear; it was hard to tell the difference.

The view reminded me of the first time I rode the bus to school. I remembered looking back at my house for as long as I could, watching it shrink smaller and smaller as the bus rolled farther down the street until my house finally vanished.

Before I knew it, the ground below disappeared behind the pure white of the clouds. The ship picked up even more speed, which pinned me to the seat. Mrs. Sosa and Mom had described what it would feel like, but it was much stronger than I had imagined. I was completely stuck to my seat. Everything felt really heavy. I couldn't even lift my head to see Cozzie. I squeezed his hand a little harder, and he squeezed back. "It's okay, Starr," he said. I felt like crying for so many reasons. I was leaving everything behind, and I was really, *really* scared.

Soon we reached a height where Earth didn't look

like a flat surface anymore. It was round, and I could see the black of space surrounding it. All the training in the world couldn't have prepared me for how beautiful it appeared. The intense pressure I had felt had faded away and the feeling of falling I had felt in the simulator returned. Since I had experienced it before, I got used to it pretty quickly. I was glad I hadn't had much to eat before we left because my stomach was doing a dance.

I snapped a picture and sent it to Allison and Tia. None of us said anything for what seemed like a really long time. Finally, Mom broke the silence. "Well, you're the first kids to *ever* go to space. What do you think?"

"It's cool!" Apollo said.

Really, I thought, *you're one of the first children to ever visit space, and the best you can come up with is "It's cool"?*

I waited, trying to think of the perfect thing to say, but I couldn't think of anything. Dad's camera was on me, and I was feeling a lot of pressure to say the perfect thing. "I don't know," I finally said.

"I agree with Starr," Dad said. "There aren't words to describe it."

"How about you, Cozzie?" Mom asked. "What are your thoughts about being the youngest person to ever go to space?"

Cozzie leaned as far forward as he could to see the view. Then he leaned all the way to his right, and then all the way to his left. "No aliens . . . yet, but I'm looking."

Chapter 7

HELLO DOWN THERE

Below us, the blue of Earth stretched out and curved off into the deepest black of space. It looked a lot different from photographs I'd seen. The clouds swirled far below us and reminded me of cotton candy. A thin layer, which reminded me of water, wrapped around the planet just above the ground.

"Earth looks like a gigantic water droplet," I said.

"That's an interesting way to describe it, because in a lot of ways it is like a gigantic water droplet," Mom said.

"What if someone eats it?" Cozzie asked. "Like we ate the water drops when we had space school."

"No one is going to eat Earth," Dad reassured him.

"Earth isn't really a water droplet," Mom said, "but it's a lot like one. The surface is made up of mostly water."

"What's that thin layer between the land and space?" Apollo asked.

"That's the atmosphere," Mom answered. "It contains all the gases we need to breathe, the clouds, the weather — all of it. Without the atmosphere, we wouldn't be able to live on the planet."

"Cool!" he said.

"If you think that's cool, just wait. Space is full of cool."

Mom pushed the thrusters and the ship cruised forward. I could read the numbers on the dashboard. We were 250 miles above Earth's surface. Even though it didn't feel like we were moving very fast, the speedometer read 17,159 miles per hour!

"What's that line where the light stops?" Apollo asked, pointing to a place on Earth where it looked like daylight and night met.

"That's the line where daylight ends and night begins. Where we are right now is facing the Sun, but on the other side of the planet, it's night."

We were moving so fast that a few minutes later the Sun had vanished behind Earth and everything below us was in darkness.

"How come we can still see the clouds if it's nighttime?" Apollo asked.

"The Moon," I said. "The moonlight is shining on the clouds."

"It's actually the sunlight reflecting off the Moon onto Earth," Mom said. "Even though the Sun is on the other side of the planet right now, the Moon is so high up that the Sun's light hits the Moon. It's how we see the Moon at night when we're on Earth. The Moon doesn't make its own light; it's being lit up by the Sun."

Earth at night was my new favorite thing. The way the lights from the cities and towns glowed was so beautiful. I clicked another picture, typed *Hello down there,* and texted it to Allison and Tia.

Tia texted right back: *So beautiful!! So jealous!!*

Allison didn't get back to me.

Suddenly, a neon-green light appeared to be dancing on top of the atmosphere.

"ALIENS!" Cozzie shouted.

"Those are the Northern Lights," Mom said. "When charged particles from the Sun strike atoms and molecules in Earth's atmosphere, they excite those atoms, causing them to light up."

"Can you explain it without all the science words?" Apollo asked.

"It's caused by the Sun," Mom said.

I was kind of amazed by how much stuff Mom knew.

"Now that you've had a little tour of the neighborhood, who's ready to check out our new home?" she asked.

Chapter 8

LIKE A TRANSFORMER

When the space station appeared in the distance, we were still on the night side of Earth. The lights on the station made it appear yellow against the black space.

"It looks like a molecule," Apollo said.

"Wow! Look who's been paying attention in science class," Dad said. Apollo always complained about school, even though he usually did pretty well.

"So, what's a molecule?" I asked Apollo.

"A molecule is a group of atoms joined together," Mom interrupted. "Atoms are the building blocks of the objects around us. The ship, your helmet, the seats are all made up of atoms. They make up everything we know in the world," she said, slowing the speed of the ship.

Apollo typed something into his phone and showed me. A picture of a molecule displayed on the screen.

"It does look like a molecule," I said, looking at the screen, then the space station. I snapped a picture and sent it to Allison and Tia.

"Mrs. Sosa designed it like that," Mom replied. "Each circular area that you see is a room, and each of the small tubes connecting the circular spaces is a hallway. On the station, we call the circular rooms pods and the hallways tubes. Every pod is connected to another by one or more tubes."

"How does it travel through space?" Apollo asked. "The shape seems kind of weird."

"The shape it's in now is perfect for orbiting. When it's time to move the station, it can change into another shape that's better for traveling."

"It's like a Transformer!" Cozzie said. "Like in the movies."

"It is a lot like a Transformer," Apollo said.

Mom pressed a button on the ship's control panel that opened a large hatch on one of the space station's pods. She slowed our speed even more, so it felt like we were in a hovering helicopter. Once our entire ship was safely inside, the hatch quickly closed.

Mom parked beside three other spaceships. I was surprised that we landed so softly. She turned off the engines and pressed a button that opened a panel on the top of the ship like a gigantic sunroof.

For a split second I held my breath, thinking I wouldn't be able to breathe. "It's safe to breathe, Starr," Mom said.

I inhaled deeply, taking my first breath of space air. It wasn't any different from the air on Earth. I wondered how there was oxygen on the station.

"How?" I asked. "Didn't all the oxygen just go out when the hatch opened?"

"When the hatch opens, the air inside the station is kept in by a force field." She took off her helmet, unbuckled, and floated gently up out of her seat. I took my helmet off too. It felt so good to finally get it off.

"Can I unbuckle now?" Apollo asked.

"Be my guest," Mom said, rising up out of the ship.

Cozzie unbuckled next. He rose up from his seat, looking down on me, and started laughing, "Look at your hair!" he shouted.

Dad turned to look at me and started laughing too. I glanced down toward my shoulders, where my hair should be, and noticed it was gone. So I reached up above my head and realized it was floating! My hair was experiencing Zero-G for the first time. On Earth and in takeoff we had to wear helmets, so I didn't get to experience how my hair would perform. It was kind of like the way your hair moves with the current of the water when you are underwater. I moved my head around and let my hair dance above me.

"Unbuckle, Starr!" Cozzie encouraged.

I released the buckle and felt my body lift. Mom had floated up to the top of the parking garage and was making her way along the ceiling toward the exit. We all followed.

Once at the top, I grabbed hold of a stabilizer bar and followed behind Mom. She led us out of the parking garage and through one of the tubes. It looked like it was made of clear glass.

I quickly realized I wouldn't be touching the ground much in my new home. We flew along the tube like superheroes until we came out into another large pod. The entire thing was clear. There wasn't anything in it, so I could still see out into space in every direction. The Moon was full in the distance. I couldn't tell what part of Earth we were over because there was a thick layer of clouds surrounding the planet's surface.

"What is this pod?" I asked Mom.

"This is the first pod you enter on the station. It's

designed to help people get used to weightlessness. From top to bottom it's over two hundred feet high. You can also appreciate the view of Earth from space. The walls are crystal clear, so you feel like you're just floating in space. Watch this," she said, clapping her hands quickly three times. The lights went out. No one made a sound. She waved for us to follow her to the bottom of the pod. We all settled slowly to the bottom, taking in the beauty of the Moon and Earth, and of the endless space beyond.

My phone buzzed.

"Be present, Starr," Cozzie said, and we all laughed.

"Go ahead," Mom said.

It was Allison: *It was great talking with you too. Thanks for calling. Talk again soon.*

I was confused, so I texted back: *Did you try to call me?*

She texted back: *OOPS! Sorry, Starr. That text was for Tia. We just got off the phone. I must have sent it in the group text by mistake. How's it going up there? Great pics!*

Why would she talk on the phone with Tia? I wondered. *Why wouldn't she want to include me in the text?* For some reason I felt a little embarrassed, even though I hadn't done anything embarrassing.

"What's wrong?" Dad asked. "You look like you've seen a ghost."

"I don't know," I said.

"Who wants to race to the top?" Dad asked. He pushed with his feet off the bottom of the pod, launching himself up like Peter Pan. Apollo followed, then Mom holding on to Cozzie. I didn't want to be the only one at the bottom, so I pushed off on the floor as hard as I could and launched myself. I couldn't catch up to them, but I didn't mind because it was so awesome soaring like an eagle through the pod. I closed my eyes and tried to be present, imagining I was a fairy with wings and glittery sparkles trailing off behind me.

Chapter 9

AQUAPONICS

Mom led us through another tube. We came out in a pod so brightly lit I had to cover my eyes as I floated in.

"Fish!" Cozzie shouted.

He was right. The pod was like a gigantic aquarium. Fish were enclosed in huge tanks. On top of the tanks, someone was growing lots of flowers and green plants!

"This is one of the most exciting rooms on the station," Mom said. "It's our aquaponics farm. It'll help provide us with oxygen and food."

I could see plants with tomatoes, cucumbers, lettuce,

and all kinds of other vegetables. A woman with short, reddish hair appeared from behind a bunch of plants.

"Hi, Kathy!" Mom said. "Kids, Kathy is an old friend of mine and runs the aquaponics pod. She's a master at growing plants in space and is a big part of how we can all survive up here for long periods of time."

"Hi, kids. I've heard all about you. Welcome to space!"

"Thanks!" Cozzie and I said at the same time. We giggled.

"How do you have fish in space?" I asked.

"The fish are in special tanks designed to keep the water from floating out. The plants grow above the tanks, allowing the roots to take in water and nutrients without soil. The plants produce oxygen, which is pumped throughout the station for us to breathe. Then it's pumped back into the tanks to keep the fish alive. It's a system that fuels itself."

I didn't understand most of what Kathy had said, but it seemed pretty amazing. Cozzie floated up to one of

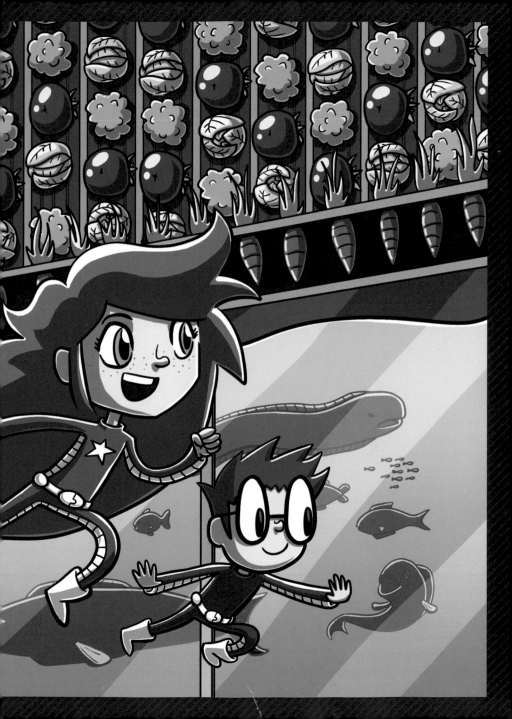

the tanks and pressed his face against the glass. "Can I name them?" he asked.

"There are a few hundred fish in here, sweetheart. That's a lot of names," Kathy said.

"I don't mind."

"Then be my guest. You can be in charge of naming the fish."

"Yay!" Cozzie shouted, and immediately he began naming the fish. "That one is Michael, and that one is Meredith, and that one is Toby . . ."

I realized that he was naming them after the kids in his class. I guess he wasn't the only one missing his friends.

Kathy led us around the pod, and it was completely amazing.

"The plants don't always know which way to grow because of microgravity," Kathy explained. "I use light to help train them to grow in the direction I want."

"My class did an experiment in school where we grew

plants in a box," I said. "We cut a hole in the box and shined a light through the hole. Over a few weeks, we learned that the plants grew toward the hole where the light shined."

"That's a lot like what I'm doing up here. Sounds like you'll make a great helper."

"I'd love to help out," I said. "I love gardening and animals."

"I'm going to stay in here all the time," Cozzie said.

"I'm glad you're excited to help, but you have a whole lot more to see," Mom said.

My phone buzzed. It was Tia: *Hi, Starr. I called Allison a little while ago to ask her a question. I hope you don't mind. How's it going up there? Keep the pictures coming.*

I felt really confused and left out. What were they talking about? They didn't even know each other.

"Starr, let's take a break from the phone," Dad said.

"Can I just text Tia and Allison back quickly?"

"Please wait a little while," Mom said. "We just got here."

Our next stop was the machine room. There we met a man named Professor Will. He was really tall and super-skinny. He had one of those handlebar moustaches that curled up on each side.

"You guys are going to travel all over the solar system, and my job is to build whatever machines we might need to help make the missions safe and fun for all of us. I actually have a new invention that I've been working on that I think you guys are going to love. I know you've only been on the station for a short time, but have you noticed that you have to do a lot of pushing off of things and holding onto bars?"

We all nodded. "Right! I've developed this little gadget that I think you guys will appreciate," the professor continued. "It's a cruiser. It works a lot like a fan, but it has handles on each side. It will help move you from place to place in the station without all the pushing off and holding onto stabilizer bars."

He gave each of us a device that looked a lot like a

large spotlight. It reminded me of the devices I'd seen scuba divers use on nature shows. Each handle had a throttle like a motorcycle. When I twisted the throttle back, the cruiser took off, pulling me behind it. "How do I steer?" I asked, feeling out of control.

"Lean to your left to go left and to your right to go right," he said over the low hum of the cruiser. When I gave this a try, it was so easy to use. All I had to do was lean a little and the cruiser turned.

"This is awesome!" Apollo shouted.

After a few minutes of zipping around the machine room, Mom waved us all in. "Let's leave the cruisers here with Professor Will, and we can come back and practice another time. We still have so much more to see."

We thanked the professor and followed Mom down the next tube. My phone buzzed again, but I ignored it.

Chapter 10

DANCING ON THE CEILING

My room was a clear pod like the others, but it was full of all my stuff. It was super-big and split up into lots of smaller sections that were like little nooks.

"Follow me," Mom said, pushing off toward a small area loaded with stuffed animals.

She pressed a button that opened a hatch and then she lowered herself inside. I followed in awe.

"All of your stuffed animals are in here," Mom said, gently pushing an armful of stuffed animals my way. "We've even added a few new ones."

Stuffed animals floated all around me. There must have been a hundred of them. It reminded me of going in the ball pit at the play gym when I was really little. I wrapped a giant stuffed owl in my arms and let the others soar by.

"This is amazing!" I said, snapping a picture. Beyond the stuffed animals, I noticed a giant purple square built into the side of the sphere. "What's in the purple square?" I asked Mom.

"Let's find out!" she exclaimed.

A few moments later, we entered through a hatch in the side, and I instantly knew what it was. A beautiful wooden dance floor like the one they have at my dance school ran along the floor, up the walls on three sides, and across the ceiling! Mom opened a compartment and took out my ballet shoes.

"No way!" I said. I had them on in no time, and before I knew it, I was dancing up the walls and across the ceiling. It was out of this world!

If that wasn't enough, there was a section with a massive telescope and a computer, another filled with all my toys, and finally the best part of the whole thing: my bed.

My bed was unlike anything I'd ever seen before. It was like a gigantic egg built into the pod. I followed Mom through the hatch in the side and found myself inside the coziest little nook. The entire space was lined with what felt like a feather blanket. It had a little night-light, a bunch of soft pillows, and plenty of room to stretch out and sleep. "This is amazing!" I said.

"Check this out," Mom said, clicking another button. The soft blanket liner pulled back on one side, revealing a beautiful view of space.

"Look at all those stars," I said.

"Do you like it?" Mom asked hopefully.

"I love it!" I exclaimed. "Thank you."

"I'm glad," Mom said. "I should be thanking you, though. You were right when you said this was my dream. The thing you didn't realize at the time was that you're a big part of that dream." She gave me a squeeze. "It means so much to me that you're giving it a try. I know it's hard leaving home and Allison, but I'm sure everything is going to work out. Sometimes these things just need a little time. Trust me."

"I love you, Mom," I said.

"I love you too, Starr." Mom smiled.

"Mom, I think Tia and Allison are going to become friends. I think they talked on the phone and didn't want me to know."

She looked surprised. "What makes you think that?"

I showed her the texts.

"I think you need some rest," Mom said. "Why don't you take a little time to yourself and catch up with us a little later?"

She left, and for the first time, I was alone in space. Below, I could make out that we were directly over India. I pushed up against the window. There were hardly any clouds and the lights of the cities sparkled like diamonds. I wondered if anyone down there was looking up and could see the station. Maybe someone at that very moment could see our station and was wondering if it was a plane or a star or an alien spaceship. My eyelids felt so heavy.

I must have fallen asleep, because the next thing I knew I was looking at the sunrise. The light shimmered off an endless blue that I figured was the Pacific Ocean. I couldn't tell if I had been asleep for five minutes or five hours. Within a few minutes the sunlight was so bright I had to close the viewing hatch. My sleeping egg went completely dark. *This must be what a chick feels like,* I thought.

I checked my messages. The first one was from Tia: *Hi, Starr! How's it going up there? I just wanted to say good luck, and I'm sorry if you were upset that I called Allison. You've told me so much about her during training. I figured I should get to know her too.*

There was also a message from Allison: *Hi, Starr.*

Sorry if I've been weird. I've just been really upset about losing you. Things aren't the same here. Have fun.

I felt a little better that they texted me, but I was still a little worried about them becoming friends. They were down on Earth, while I was way up in space. What if they realized they didn't need me anymore?

I opened the hatch and floated out into my room, stretching like I always do after I get out of bed. A good stretch after a nap is always nice, but stretching in space was amazing. I floated in midair with a full stretch. I slowly twisted and twirled, and it felt like a dream.

I made my way to the exit tube that leads out into the rest of the station. I could hear laughing coming from a tube entrance. It sounded like my brothers. I floated in, and they were playing what looked like dodgeball with Dad.

There were colorful foam balls floating everywhere. Apollo wound up and hurled a ball my way. I dodged it just in time, laughing.

Chapter 11

SPACE WALK

The whole family spent our first week playing and getting used to life on the station. We had to relearn how to do just about everything. Eating, washing, and even going to the bathroom were bizarre new challenges in space.

One week after we arrived, it was the day of our first space walk, and I couldn't wait. It was also Allison's birthday. I texted her to say "Happy Birthday," and she texted back thanking me. I tried to call her, but she didn't answer. I left a message and sang "Happy Birthday" to her.

I hadn't talked with her for a few days before that. We had texted a few times, and she didn't seem mad anymore, but something still seemed strange. I worried that she and Tia were going to become best friends. Maybe Mom and Dad were right, and I just needed to give things some time.

Professor Will was making last-minute adjustments to our space suits. He attached an elastic cord to each of us. Each suit was super-thick and had a big glass helmet that fit on top and covered the whole head. I felt like a robot.

"How long are we going to be outside the station?" I asked.

"It's really up to you," the professor replied. "We'll be in constant contact, so just let me know when you've had enough."

I felt kind of bad for Cozzie because he was too young to go on the space walk. He was staying behind with Kathy. Dad, Mom, Apollo, and I were the only ones going.

"Are you sure you'll be all right?" I asked him. "We won't be gone long."

"I'll be fine. Kathy said I can help her take care of the fish."

"We still have a few hundred more of them to name," Kathy said, giving me a wink.

Cozzie tugged on Kathy's arm and whispered something to her. They both smiled and Kathy put her finger to her lips, as though they had a secret.

"What is it?" I asked.

"Nothing," Kathy said. "Cozzie has a little surprise for you guys when you get back."

"What?" Apollo asked.

"You'll have to wait to find out," Cozzie said, mischievously.

"I hate to break this up," Professor Will said, "but the conditions are perfect. We need to get you folks out of here."

Cozzie and Kathy took off on her cruiser together.

"What is Cozzie up to?" I asked Dad. He just shrugged and tried to look like he didn't know, but I could tell he did.

Professor Will led us to an area in the far back of the transportation room. He pointed to a set of doors, saying, "These may look like elevator doors you'd see back on Earth, but it's actually an exit. You should not go near it unless you are with me and in your space suits. Do you understand?"

We nodded. He pushed a key into a slot in the wall and the doors slid open.

"As I mentioned, it looks a lot like an elevator, but you'll see that there is a second set of doors on the back wall. Once you are inside, and I've safely closed these doors, I'll open the back doors and you guys will be free to safely float out of the station."

We floated into the elevator, and then the first set of doors closed behind us.

"Opening the doors in 3, 2, 1. Have fun!" Professor

Will said. The back doors of the elevator opened, and then there was nothing between us and open space except for the elastic cord. Apollo kicked off the station's wall and floated out. I followed, and then came Dad and Mom.

My heart felt like a drum beating in my chest.

"Starr, are you alright?" Professor Will asked through the speakers in my helmet. "Your heart rate is sky high."

"I'm fine," I said. "It's just the most exciting thing ever!"

Professor Will asked, "Do you notice how amazingly quiet it is in space?"

He was right. I'd never heard such quiet. Everything seemed so still. Earth rolled slowly beneath us. I could hear myself breathing and felt the thump of my heart slow to a steadier beat.

I could see Earth and the Moon at the same time. The stars were brighter than I'd ever seen before.

"I'm turning on the smart glass in your helmets," Professor Will said.

Suddenly, wherever I looked, I saw each star's name appear next to it.

"If you want to know anything about a particular star or planet you see, simply ask and the computer in your helmet will tell you. Give it a try," said the professor.

"Where is Mars?" I asked.

"Turn slightly to your left," a computer voice answered. "It will be the reddish-looking star."

I turned to my left, and there it was.

"Would you like me to magnify your view?" the computer asked.

"Yes!" I said. The view zoomed in on Mars, and all the other images and words vanished. I could see Mars so clearly. It looked a little bit like a tiny, red moon.

We must have been out on our walk for about an hour when I noticed a ship cruise toward the station. It slowed by the landing pod and vanished inside.

"Who's in the ship?" Apollo asked.

"It's a supply delivery," Mom said. "Let's go and see what's arrived."

ALIENS FROM ANOTHER PLANET

When we got back inside the ship, we took off our suits. "Hey," Dad said, looking at his phone. "This is weird."

"What is it?" I asked.

"Take a look for yourself." He held out a picture on his phone of a smiling Cozzie between two aliens! Their long, oval faces were scaly and green. Their large eyes gave me the creeps. The picture was only of their heads, so I couldn't see their bodies at all.

"What is that?" I asked.

"It looks like Cozzie captured a couple of creatures from another planet," Mom said, smiling.

"I knew aliens were real!" Apollo said. "We need to find Cozzie!"

I was super-confused.

"Can we use a couple of cruisers?" Mom asked Professor Will.

He pointed to them. "Be my guests."

We all grabbed a cruiser and followed Mom through the exit tube. We cruised from pod to pod looking for Cozzie. I knew that he and Kathy were probably playing a game. Apollo probably thought it was two actual aliens, but he didn't seem too worried about them eating his brain.

When we finally found Cozzie, he was in his room playing dodgeball with the two aliens!

"What's happening?" Apollo asked.

"I'm playing with aliens!" Cozzie said through uncontrollable giggling. "I told you there would be aliens in space."

Looking at them, I knew they weren't *real* aliens, but people wearing alien masks.

"What's going on?" I asked Mom.

"I told you to give things some time and they'd work out," she smirked.

One of the figures pulled off the mask. "Tia!" I shouted. "What are you doing here?"

"I couldn't let you have all the fun," she said. "I had to come and check it out for myself. Also, my grandmother said it was my job to make sure you have whatever you need up here. I brought you what I knew you missed most."

I thought about what I missed most. "Allison?" I asked hopefully.

"Nope. It's a very dangerous alien," Cozzie said. "Don't get too close! It will eat all of your brains!"

The alien slowly took off the mask. "Allison!" I shouted as I cruised over to her as fast as I could. "What are you doing here? I thought you were mad at me."

"I was at first, until Tia called and told me how much you missed me. She helped me realize how unfairly I was treating you when you moved. It's not your fault you had to go."

Tia floated over. "You did that for me?" I asked her.

"That's what partners do," Tia said.

"I'm so sorry," Allison said. "Do you forgive me?"

"Of course," I said. "I just can't believe you're really here! Hey, it's your birthday!"

"I know," Allison said.

"You're the first girl to ever have a birthday in space," I said.

"Hey, you're probably right!" she said, smiling.

"You're not going to become famous and forget all about me, are you?" I asked sarcastically.

"Very funny," she said. "You're my best friend. I'll never forget about you."

We hugged. "Come on," I said. "We have a party to plan."

ABOUT THE AUTHOR

Raymond Bean is the best-selling author of the *Benji Franklin*, *Sweet Farts*, and *School Is a Nightmare* books. He teaches by day and writes by night. He lives in New York with his wife, two children, and a Cockapoo named Lily. His bags are packed for the day when space-cations become a reality.

ABOUT THE ILLUSTRATOR

Matthew Vimislik is an illustrator and game designer working in Rochester, NY. He lives with his wife, two cats, and possibly a family of Black-billed Cuckoo birds that has made a nest in his meticulously preened hair.

STARR'S GUIDE TO SPACE TRAVEL

APOLLO — My mom and dad named my older brother Apollo after the Apollo space missions that landed the first humans on the Moon.

AQUAPONICS — Fish and plants live together in an aquaponic system. That means a place where fish and plants are grown together. The fish waste provides nutrients to the plants, and the plants help purify the water. It's how we grow food and raise fish on our space station.

ATMOSPHERE — The layers of gas that surround a planet. Earth's atmosphere is made up of five main layers.

ATOM — An atom is a super-small amount of something. Tiny particles called atoms are the building blocks of all matter. They can be combined with other atoms to form molecules.

COSMO — My little brother's name is Cosmo. Mom and Dad got his name from the word "cosmos," which means "the universe." It's a good name because sometimes my brother thinks the universe revolves around him.

DOCUMENTARY FILM — My dad makes documentary films. They're films about real things or people. He's made some real snoozers.

MICROGRAVITY — The word "micro" means very small. Gravity is the force that holds us to the ground. In space, gravity is not as strong, so "microgravity" basically means "small gravity." When you see astronauts floating around in space, it's because of microgravity. Microgravity is so much fun! You have to experience it one day!

MOLECULE — A molecule is two or more atoms joined together. Water is a great example of a molecule. It's made up of two hydrogen atoms and one oxygen atom. Our space station was designed to look like a molecule.

ORBIT — The way something goes around an object in space is called its orbit. The Moon is in orbit around Earth.

SIMULATOR — A machine used for training. Mrs. Sosa trained us for space in a Zero-G simulator. It was amazing!

SPACE-CATION — Tia and I pretty much made the word up. It's basically the words "space" and "vacation" put together.

STABILIZER — A stabilizer is used to keep something steady or stable. In space we use them to hold us in place. If we didn't have them, we'd float all over the place!

ZERO-G — This is basically the same thing as microgravity, when you don't feel gravity and you float. Sometimes people call this weightlessness. Most people think of it as floating, but it feels more like you are falling.

FAR-OUT QUESTIONS

1   Space travel may be possible for all people one day. If you had the opportunity to visit space, would you go? What would be your biggest concern? What would you be most excited to see or experience? Compare your response to Starr's. How are your feelings similar to or different from Starr's?

2   *Out of This World* is told from Starr's perspective. If you could tell the story from another character's perspective, which character would you choose? How do you feel that character's perspective might be different from Starr's?

3   Some people are planning to attempt to colonize space in the future. Do you think people will ever be able to colonize space successfully? What do you think are the biggest challenges to colonizing space? Do you think Starr and the rest of the crew could continue living in space? Include examples from the book to support your answer.

INTERGALACTIC IDEAS

1   When Starr learns she's moving to space, she is upset. She worries that the move will ruin her and Allison's friendship. If you could talk with Starr, what advice would you give her?

2   Starr and her family raise fish and grow plants for food. If you were in charge of the aquaponics system on the space station, what plants would you grow? What challenges do you think you might face growing your food in space?

3   Starr's room has her own dance studio! She quickly learns dancing in space is way different from dancing on Earth. She can actually dance on the walls and the ceiling! If you lived on a space station and could design your own special room, what would it be like? What activities would you want to do in microgravity?

Check out some *space-tastic* websites at www.FactHound.com

Just type in the book ID: 9781496536174
and prepare to blast off!